A Bicycle from Bridgetown

McGRAW-HILL BOOK COMPANY
New York St. Louis San Francisco

from Bridgetown

by Dawn C. Thomas

Illustrated by Don Miller

Library of Congress Cataloging in Publication Data

Thomas, Dawn C
A bicycle from Bridgetown.

SUMMARY: Edgar dreams of having a bicycle like those of the famous Bridgetown cyclists.
[1. Bicycles and bicycling—Fiction. 2. Barbados—Fiction] I. Miller, Don, 1923- ill. II. Title.
PZ7.T3664Bi [Fic] 75-2141
ISBN 0-07-064255-9 lib. bdg.

1 2 3 4 5 6 7 BPBP 9 8 9 8 7 6 5

To mom and dad, Eleanor Gill, and the late Conrad Gill:
It was your memories of the island, Barbados, that gave you the strength, wisdom, and courage to shape the impossible dream for us in a new country where you had no roots.

With love,
Dawn for Marjorie and Jean

GRE
YOUR

The afternoon sun was a ball of red and gold, shining so brightly that its strong rays beat through the tan metal roof of the bus. Some of the passengers sat with their eyes closed, dozing to its jerking rhythm, while others shifted their heads from side to side, watching the cane cutters in the fields of the many plantations close to the road.

Edgar squirmed in his seat behind Moodis, the driver. *If I was taller*, he thought, *I'd be able to see over Moodis' shoulders, and if I was stronger I'd be able to make a good wage working on the fishing boats. Oh well*, he sighed, *each day I grow older*. He shifted, keeping a tight grip on the package he held on his knees.

Beep! Beep! Moodis sounded the horn as they rounded a curve, and suddenly there were no more fields of cane or big yards filled with canna and lemon trees. Now houses were crowded side by side. And everywhere Edgar looked, people filled the streets, some crowding the doorways of shops, others loaded down with packages and shopping bags, pushing their way from sidewalk vendor to sidewalk vendor.

A shout went up in the bus. "There they are!" Heads popped out of windows and some people stood to get a better view.

The Barbados bicycling team pedaled by, strong brown legs pumping up and down, moving the bikes with easy rhythm. The chrome spokes of the racers gleamed in the sun. Each man was looking good and knew it.

Edgar closed his eyes. He could not look at them for another second. Oh, to have such a bike. And for a while, he pretended he was

on the road riding, feeling the wind whip his legs and face, knowing that those wheels could take him anywhere. Freedom was a bike!

"Bridgetown! Last stop!" Moodis called.

People started to move, hurrying out to the markets and the little rows of houses that dotted the town.

"Say," Moodis said to Edgar as he stood up, "what are you doing in town at this time of day?"

"Well, today was one of those days for mommy. She missed the boats at the Garrison. And they were moving so fast because of the loads they carried that she missed them at Speightstown, too. She wanted some cassava flour and guinea corn. You can buy those things only in town. Thomas is helping the men to mend the nets for tomorrow's fishing. Martin is working on the glass-bottom boats. So, I was the only one left to help."

"Can't believe that you would give up a swim and a soccer game on a day like today, just to market for your mother!"

"Don't mind coming to Bridgetown," Edgar murmured.

"Truth now, friend," Moodis said the words kindly. "Maybe you need someone to talk to! No trouble I hope!"

"No trouble." Edgar paused. *Maybe*, he thought, *I can tell my secret to Moodis.*

He's a good friend and . . . why, he's almost a brother.

"Listen, Moodis, every chance I get, I go where I can see them." Edgar pointed to the members of the team who had left their bikes at the curb and were now gathered around the soda shop.

"Well, boy," Moodis too was excited, "I once wished to be one of them. They are always looking good, man. And every man-child on the island of Barbados rides with them in his dreams."

"It is the bike that I dream on," Edgar said softly.

"THE BIKE!" Moodis shook his head.

"Oh, yes!" Edgar smiled. "To me those silver spokes are wings. Why I could fly from St. Lucy to St. James to Bridgetown to . . . to . . . I can earn my way with a wheel," Edgar declared. "Everybody in my family works. With a bike I could go from beach club to beach club and sell my coral pictures to the tourists. And oh! What fun I could have!"

"But, boy, such a thing is big money! Big, big money! Only a man can earn big money for such a big thing. And you, Edgar, are but a boy. Why," Moodis shook his head, "those are no ordinary bikes. One of those machines can bring a man fame. And a man can make money with such a machine."

"I have saved one dollar in U.S. money," Edgar said proudly.

"Good! Good! For you will need many, many dollars for such a dream. Good luck, Edgar."

Moodis got up and left the bus. He had to clock in at the depot and already he was six minutes behind schedule.

Getting late. Better get up some speed, Edgar thought as he ran out of the bus and through the streets to the market. Even a good friend like Moodis could not, would not understand. In minutes he passed the nut-sellers—women who came from Bridgetown from the eleven parishes of Barbados to sell candies, peanuts planted and picked from their gardens, and homemade goodies;

sometimes they brought along sliced leaves of banana bread or coconut cakes.

He liked the nutsellers, with their brightly colored dresses. And even on the hottest of days you could find a lady wearing a felt hat or some item of clothing, a gift from an American relative that made her stand out in the crowd. Edgar especially liked the nut-sellers who sold their wares from large trays atop their heads. *Not easy to walk with a load on your head*, he thought. And he remembered that everytime he had tried to imitate the walk, head erect, feet moving with firmly planted steps, the tray would fall.

He pushed himself to move faster and his strong brown legs helped him to fly by the fish cleaners: some sitting, some standing behind their orange-crate stands, all waiting to scale and clean the fish people bought from the boats.

At last he came to the main market area, a series of neat stands, some filled with fruits and vegetables, such as mangoes, avocados,

coconuts, and little dark brown stubs of potatoes, called "eddoes." Clusters of big green bananas hung by wires on the metal screening enclosing the large square. And everywhere he could see the market officials in crisply starched khaki uniforms, their heads protected from the hot sun by pith helmets; patrolling, keeping order, and checking to see that the weights were true and the food fresh and clean.

Finally his long legs raced him to the spot where Wilson had his grocery stand. He knew it would be faster for Wilson to read the list and gather the things.

"Well, sir," said Wilson, working swiftly with his only hand, "you must be having much company, or is your mother starting up her holiday cooking? She bought plenty by me early in the day. Not any of these, of course," he said, pointing to Edgar's neatly wrapped pile.

"What!" Edgar shook his head. "Are you sure for certain that it was my mother who was here today?"

Edgar was puzzled. How come his mother shopped twice in the same day? *MMMMmmmmmm!* Come to think of it, lately his mother had been sending him to Bridgetown, and the shopping never amounted to much. *I wonder . . . . Maybe she knows. Maybe she really knows!*

"Hurry, son," Wilson warned, "no eyeing the sights, or else you will miss the last of the boats and I see your mother has fish on this list."

With the green sack resting on his shoulder, Edgar flew across the wide street, ducking a big old chauffeur-driven Bentley and a Toyota whose driver had left it parked in the middle of the road. He darted past the shop where the team had gathered, then leaped over the railing leading down to the boats.

"Dolphin here! Shark here! Bonita here! Flying fish here! Snapper here!" Fishermen just in with fresh catches shouted to shoppers nearby in the market.

Edgar smiled to himself. *Glad there's lots*

of fish. Now I can eat as much as I want. He raced through the market to the stall with the flying fish.

"Big hurry, eh, Eddie?" Payne Clarke, a market official waved. He stood near the rows of women scaling and gutting fish for

the big hotels. Edgar waved, but kept on moving.

He eased his way over to the wire screen, where he could yell out his order. He shouted again and again before the fishman nodded his head to show he had heard.

"Thought I'd never get my fish," Edgar said as the man handed him his package.

The big clock near the square showed there were fifteen minutes before the next bus left town.

"Just time," Edgar whispered to the wind. He threaded his way in and out of the walkers who took up the street, looking at shop windows or stopping to talk with each other.

Made it. Out of breath, Edgar pressed his face to the window of the Bridgetown Bicycle and Parts Shop to get a better view of the beautiful, sleek European and American bikes on display. There were all kinds and all sizes, and it was hard for him to believe that there could be places where little children enjoyed the pleasure of riding bikes.

Mr. Connell, the manager and owner of the shop, looked up from his work. "Mmmmm! My special friend," he called, getting up and coming outside. "Hello, Edgar! I see you are once again dreaming on these bikes. One day, maybe one day . . ."

"Indeed, sir," Edgar answered. "It will be some big day in my life when I can buy a bike from your shop."

"One day, I bet you will do it. And with those fine legs of yours, you might even win a spot on the team."

Ding! Dong! Ding! Dong! The chimes of the clock in the square began to toll the hour. Suddenly, people with bundles and shopping bags and a few women with baskets atop their heads started to run in the direction of the bus depot.

"Don't want to miss my bus or the chance of getting a seat either! See you again, Mr. Connell."

Edgar began to run. He moved swiftly and, since he was quicker than most, he was lucky enough to get his favorite seat, just behind the driver. Holding his packages, he closed his eyes to think about the bikes on the long ride home.

The bus bounced its way around the bends and curves that were Highway One, and every now and then a friend getting on or getting off would poke Edgar to send a greeting to his mother.

Each time the bus stopped, Edgar shifted impatiently in his seat. *If I had my own bike*, he thought, *I could be home by now.* And he sat watching the early evening shadows settle on the fields, then across the hood of the bus. It was dark by the time he reached St. Lucy.

"Just in time, Eddie," his mother called as she saw him come through the front yard. "Maybe you can cool off with a swim. Town tends to make you hot." His mother, a wide straw hat on her head and an apron that was all pink and red and green flowers, stood in front of a tiny stove stirring an okra, yam, and codfish stew.

"See you've been busy." Edgar pinched a tiny piece off the loaf of banana bread cooling on the kitchen shelf.

"Looks like you didn't forget one thing on that list," said his mother as she checked the contents of the packages.

"No, Mommy, I think I got it all. And I got

a chance to ride with Moodis. Mustn't forget to tell Edith. She has the softs for Moodis. Sometimes he takes her for rides on his motorbike."

"As if I didn't know, little sir." Edgar's mother winked her right eye. "Your brothers are in the back funnin' as usual. I am going to clean these fish out front where I can cool off."

She moved toward the door with a pan of water and lime juice and her good cutting blade. "By the way," she turned to ask, "did you enjoy your trip to town?"

"To be sure, Mommy. Even had time to stop by the bike shop." Edgar's voice was low.

Mother tossed her head, threw the fish into the pan, and went into the front yard. From there she could call out to her friends who passed by on their way home from the cane fields and from town.

"Was town crowded?" Martin asked the question, coming into the house from the back yard. He carried a basket of newly picked okra and a few small tomatoes. It was his job each day to get the ripened fruit and vegetables from the garden.

"Sure, town was crowded."

"Did you buy us any candy?" Thomas, who was following on his brother's heels, flopped into a chair and stretched out his legs.

"Say, boy, did you give me any money for candy?"

"We're going swimming," Martin announced. "We've been waiting for you."

"Hurry along now," Thomas said, slipping past Edgar and beaning him on the head. "It is not polite to keep your elders waiting."

"Especially working elders!" Martin always had the last word.

Thomas pushed Martin and Martin shoved Edgar. Then Martin's foot caught in the rung of the chair. *Clump! CRASH!* Rushing to right the chair before his mother ran in from her fish cleaning, Thomas bumped into the table and it hit the floor with a bang.

It was Edgar who spotted the long, lean switch in his mother's hand as she hurried through the door. Martin and Thomas were too tangled in the chair and the table to dart out of her way. Edgar jumped through the window, and bending low under the windowsill, he listened to the action.

"Time and again, I've warned you boys about breaking up the furniture of this house. But no," his mother beat the air with the switch, "it is always some silly thing to start this breaking up to go on."

"Yowie!" Martin shouted, darting from side to side.

"Flogging tires me, but it teaches you!"

"I'll be good. I'll be good," Thomas promised.

Make more noise than anything else, Edgar thought. For his mother gave them no more than light taps on their legs and most of the time he wondered why she used up so much strength just to chase them.

Hope mommy forgets about looking for me. He said a silent prayer and waited for

his brothers. In a short time they staggered through the door out into the hot night air.

"Bet that cool water is going to feel better than ever," Edgar called as he followed them.

Thomas and Martin didn't stop to answer. They ran across the road and down a slope to the beach. By the time the three brothers reached their friends, the trouble of funnin' was long forgotten.

"Foolishness, nuh?" Martin laughed and pointed to Prentice Bond who stood wearing his mask and snorkel practicing underwater breathing in the sand.

"Maybe the boy has supersonic vision and can see things in the dark," Edgar giggled.

"Haven't seen that Prentice Bond's full bare face for a long time now," Martin said.

"Lucky for you," Thomas added.

"Ho, boy! That's the truth!" agreed Martin.

"Almost time for the carnival," Emerson Welch said as he came up to the brothers. "Sure wish I could make it to Trinidad."

"Well," laughed Edgar, looking at his brothers, "we just had jump up and *juve* at our house."

"Sure do miss the carnival, man." Emerson did not catch what Edgar was saying.

"Ho! Boys!" A new voice bellowed.

The boys turned to see Nugent Cumberbatch strutting toward the group, flexing his muscles and turning his head from side to side to see who might be watching him.

"Here comes the peacock," said Thomas.

"I heard you boys talking of carnival. It is hardly likely that you could miss it, as you have never seen it." He swung his shoulders. "Remember, I was the one to dance from here to Bridgetown with the big mask on my face and the finest of purple satin suits Mistress Gilkes could stitch. Ah, but it's sad," he said thoughtfully, "it's all over. Now there is no more carnival to herald the coming of Lent."

"Race you to the water!" Thomas gave the challenge.

And suddenly sand flew and feet flew and

boys were plopping like dolphins into the cool blue water, now turned to a deep purple in the moonlight. *Splash! Splash! Splash!* Small sparkling drops of water leaped into the darkness as they headed for the raft.

Edgar was strong and a good swimmer. He struck out on his own until he felt he was alone. Then, rolling onto his back, he floated and looked up at the stars. *There's the little dipper and the big dipper. Mmmmm! Better to wish on a star than to tell anyone my dream!* Now he spotted the belt of Orion and Pegasus, the winged horse. Finally, he spotted his favorite, Leo the lion. *Mmmmmm. Maybe I can find a group of stars that make a bike!*

"Ouch!" Edgar felt someting pull at his toe, and he knew it wasn't a crab or a fish. The sound of laughter told him it was Thomas. "You rotten kid! You know, man, you could send me down." And as Thomas tried to dart away, Edgar struck out after him.

The chase was on! With fast strokes, both

boys headed for shore, Edgar slightly behind his brother. Thomas zigzagged, dived, and popped his head up every now and then to whistle and taunt Edgar with chants.

As Thomas came close to shore, his hand hit the sand, and knowing his brother was just a whiff behind him, he stood up to run the rest of the way in.

"Eeeieieieieieieiei! Eeeieieieieieieiei!" Thomas yelped, then howled as a sea urchin's spine buried itself into the soft ball of his foot.

"Merciful father! The boy has caught an urchin unto himself." Martin, who was already on the beach, raced toward his brother.

"Yowieeeeeeeeeeeeeeeeee-ieee!" Thomas screamed, leaping high into the air and finally dropping in the sand in front of his friends.

"Sea urchin," Nugent said knowingly.

"Yowieeeeeeeeeee!" Thomas howled again and again.

"Hush your face, boy. It's not the first dumb thing you've done today." Edgar stood beside his brother on the beach.

"Your mother will know what to do," said Prentice sympathetically.

Lemon or lime juice
  and candle wax,
Will cool the sting
  of the urchin's attack!

The boys chanted the old rhyme over and over.

Martin and Edgar made a chair for carrying Thomas by joining their hands. Thomas held fast to each of their necks.

"Ugggggggggh!" Martin groaned in disgust. "Boy, you should be walking. For truth, I can't see how your foot could be hurt so bad. But I know your game."

"So do I," Edgar said, sighing from the weight of his brother. "Trying to pull at mommy's heart for pity."

The boys struggled into the front yard. And through the window they could see their mother slicing banana bread and placing it on their plates.

"Well, now, and look at you," she called as the boys came into the room. "So a sea urchin got you, eh, Thomas?"

Thomas shook his head, sank onto a chair, and held out the injured foot.

"Sit still, mind!" Mrs. Bowen took a candle from the cupboard, lit it, and then gave it to Martin to hold. Next she halved a lime. Then she treated Thomas' foot by first rubbing the candle drippings over the lump made by the urchin and then coating the spot with lime juice.

Shaking her head sadly, she examined her son's foot one more time before easing a clean white sock on it. "You, Thomas, are a boy for mischief. This foot of yours is bad, you know. There will be no working for you, and from the looks of it, you won't make anymore school before spring vacation. What a shame, nuh!"

Edgar looked at Martin, hoping he wouldn't laugh aloud. Not to go to school was a joy, but he could find no pleasure in nursing the pain of an urchin's sting. He would prefer his lessons.

The remaining days before spring vacation flew by. Each day Edgar and Martin raced home to give Thomas all of the school news. And on the Wednesday before Good Friday, Mrs. Bowen smiled as she checked Thomas' foot.

"Leave it to you, Thomas boy. Just as I said, your foot is good for walking as of tomorrow."

"Good thing! Good luck! Glad I won't have to lose my job."

"Yes, Thomas, it takes each of us doing a little something to keep food in our stomachs and a roof over our heads. Even when I fuss up some about the tricks you boys play, I am proud of all of you."

A couple of days later, Edgar decided to go down to the area of the big houses and beach clubs along the St. James coast. He carried his shell pictures in a shopping bag.

Have to walk, he said to himself, *no money for a bus*! He strolled along the beachfront, leaping over the high ground and rocks separating the long, winding stretch of beach. Then he came to the really big houses.

He began to look very carefully. *Wonder if I'll see old Mr. Carmichael today. Could be he'll need some help tending these yards come the next month or so. Now there's something I could set my mind to.* He stopped. *Yes*, he thought, *I'll find old Mr. Carmichael and ask if he needs any help.*

"John Carmichael is getting on in age," he remembered his mother saying only last Sunday in church.

"He is past getting on," his aunt Riva had added. "Mr. Carmichael's health is a tribute to hard work. Remember Syl?" she had said to Edgar's mother, "He was a friend of our parents. He must be more than eighty years."

Now, Edgar spotted Mr. Carmichael watering a bed of canna.

"Hi, Mr. Carmichael. The garden is looking good," he called out to his friend.

"Say, boy," Mr. Carmichael stopped watering the flowers to answer. "These are the thirstiest things I've ever put a hand to. Hope they last through this heat."

Edgar began to give news of his family, telling of his last trip to Bridgetown, and finally asking for a job.

"In truth, son, I'm sorry." Mr. Carmichael reached for a water gourd and took a long drink. "Money is getting harder and harder to come by and I don't see that I could afford to let you help me, if the pay is to come out of my own pocket." Mr. Carmichael took his handkerchief and wiped the sweat from his face and neck. "Patience, child. You'll find something to do to earn your way. You are a good boy."

Edgar thanked the old man and waved his good-bye before heading into a grove of coconut trees.

Click! Click! Splat! Edgar jumped. *Che-ee-ee. Che-ee-ee-ee.* Two monkeys chattered in a tree. They clapped their hands and laughed. *Clump! Clump!* Two coconuts hit the ground and rolled toward Edgar. The monkeys scampered off in search of their lunch.

"Some stuff!" Edgar exclaimed as he watched them chase each other across the grass, stopping every now and then to shake a scolding finger. Edgar kept an eye out as he neared the beach for bits of glass and shells and coral that might pierce his bare feet.

"Some hot day!" He wiped his face with a

palm leaf. Suddenly, his eyes caught something shiny in a thick covering of leaves. It was chrome, he could tell.

Edgar moved with speed, his hands snatching at the leaves. *Thump! Thump! Thumpity-thump!* His heart echoed like a steel drum. No! He uncovered handlebars. Yes, there it was! A bike! Spokes in good condition! And tires brand new even if the machine wasn't. *Who would leave such a bike in such a place?* he asked himself.

Edgar stood the bike up, and giving quick darting looks over each shoulder, he rolled it back and forth. *Must belong to one of the beach boys at the Colony Club. Maybe it belongs to Mr. Carmichael. Maybe someone on the beach hid the bike here for safekeeping. But maybe*, he hoped, *someone just doesn't want it!*

And as all of these thoughts raced through his mind, Edgar knew there was something strange about where he had found the bike.

A bike was as good as a car, and this bike could be sold for a small sum. He did not know what to do. He needed time to think. Carefully, he hid the bike in the palms.

If it is still here when I return, I will take a ride, he promised himself. *Maybe someone has lost it and will be willing to give a small reward to the finder*.

Slowly Edgar moved out onto the beach again. He wondered how to go about getting information on the bike. He walked, forgetting his plan to sell his shell pictures.

"Say, kid."

Edgar looked up. He had come much farther than he realized. Before him he saw a sea of people, their faces hidden by hats, and chairs and legs, and lotion and towels, and trays with glasses. He could not find the owner of the voice.

"Young man!" This time he saw a hat shaped like a small palm tree with fruit dangling on the brim bob up and down.

Edgar moved toward the hat, just as a woman unfolded from a green and white chair.

"Say, aren't you the kid with those wonderful shell pictures?"

"I do have some pictures," Edgar said shyly.

"He's the one, Erma." Another hat on the head of another woman bobbed.

Edgar spread the few pictures from his bag on the sand to let the two women judge his work.

"I'll take them all," the first voice said after one look and without asking the price.

Edgar was surprised and happy. *What luck! Today is my day.*

"They are fifty cents each," he said softly. "That is, they are fifty cents each in American money," he added.

"Fine! Fine! Very good," said the first lady again. "Can you come this way tomorrow?" She paid him.

He nodded.

"Good! I'll take what you have tomorrow, too!"

Luck! This must be a sign about the bike. He walked on.

"Look up, man! You're going to knock me down!"

Edgar felt a hand on his shoulder. It was his friend, the head waiter at the Colony.

"Ho, John! Too busy with good luck and signs to have much sense."

"So luck was good, eh?"

"Indeed! How goes it with you, John?"

"Fine to be sure." John pushed his hands deep into his pants pockets, rocking back on his heels. "I stay busy with one thing and another. Tourism is big business." He brushed an imaginary thread from his bright red jacket, then straightened his bow tie. "We try to please," he said importantly. "In my position I worry all the time. Don't want a single slip-up on my record."

"By the way," Edgar said, "can people still park their bikes in those stands?" He pointed to a wooden platform.

"Of course," John answered. "Did you leave your bike by the road?"

"I have no bike, man. Just a dream! But soon . . ." He flashed the American bills. "Besides, wouldn't that be a silly place to leave a bike?"

"Indeed! Indeed! Everybody around here puts their bikes right over there. Must go to work, now."

"And I will swim," said Edgar. "My work is over for this day."

"Enjoy life, Edgar," John said. "There is little funnin' in manhood." Then John walked away.

Edgar folded his clothes, placing them in his shopping bag. *Hope some of my friends are on the raft*, he thought, tumbling into the cool, clear blue water.

With diving and racing and stretching in the sun, the hours of the day slipped away. But all the while Edgar kept his eyes on the beach. Some of the beach sitters were now in the glass-bottom boat and he knew that others must have gone shopping in town.

From his spot on the raft, Edgar could watch the help from the houses leaving for their afternoon break. Thinking about the bike, he waited patiently for the beach boys to change shifts. Then his eyes scanned the beach and the little beach houses from which drinks and light refreshments were served. Enough time had passed. Now to see about the bike.

On his way back Edgar was not too anxious to reach the spot in the path where the bike should be. *It must surely be gone*, he thought. *I know it's gone. No use thinking about it*, he told himself.

At last he was there. Edgar forced himself to look. Why, the leaves had not been touched! Edgar poked around. Yes! It was safe. Now he wanted to ride it, but was afraid. He sat for a while. *Must check the papers tonight and listen to the talk of my friends*, he thought. *Maybe I'll find out something.*

It was not easy to be himself when each part of his body tingled with excitement. Edgar wanted to shout. He wanted to know for sure about the bike so that he could feel free to ride it.

At home, Thomas and Martin had lots to talk about. As usual, Edgar was silent. No one bothered him. For all the Bowens knew, Edgar was a dreamer.

"What's new in the paper?" Edgar asked his mother.

"Why, not too much. The new Queen Elizabeth II will be docking here in two days." She held up the paper, showing him the picture of the ship. "It will be a half-day holiday for some. And all the shops in Bridgetown will be opened."

"Indeed! Indeed! Martin and some other guys are going to be a part of the welcoming steel band," Thomas said, and stared at the picture. "Bet that is some boat."

"Anything . . . anything about any lost bicycle in the news?" Edgar asked softly.

"Did you luck up on one, boy?" Thomas shouted before his mother had a chance to say a word.

Mother eyed Thomas silently, warning him of his boldness.

"Excuse me, please!" Thomas rubbed one toe against the other.

"No, son!" she answered. Looking at Edgar, she shook her head.

"What's on for tonight?" Martin asked.

"There's a new movie in town," said Thomas. "A lot in it about New York. Moodis took Edith to see it."

"I wanted to visit with Emerson and his brothers," Martin said. "They just got some new toys from the States."

"I," mother said, "am going to church. You boys can go to the beach or sit out front. Sorry, Thomas, no money for the movies this week."

The next day after his breakfast and after the household chores had been done, Edgar raced to St. James. He ran down the path, hoping and wondering if he would find the bike. And it was still there.

Edgar could keep himself from riding the bike no longer. He jumped on and wibble-wobbled back and forth. He pedaled. He tested the handbrakes. *Good bike.* At last he was free.

The first day, Edgar rode the wheel all the

way to Bathsheba, where he saw giant waves of water, so cold it seemed frosted, whip the huge boulders and rocks as they crashed onto the sand. He weaved in and out among the Canadians who picnicked there. They were the only foreigners brave enough to try the rough waters. Edgar stopped briefly to scan the sandy coves for shells and bits of glass, but it was impossible for him to stay away from the bike for long.

Each day Edgar covered a different spot on the island. He rode to the animal caves, where for twenty-five cents he went below the ground to see fossils. One day he went all the way to Seawell Airport to watch the tourists come in. *What fun*, he thought, watching the luggage move along on the conveyor belt, and for a second or two he dreamed of places beyond his beloved Barbados.

Each night Edgar returned the wonderful bike to its hiding spot, then he would dream about it being gone in the morning. And each evening he asked his mother about the news in the paper.

Edgar sold no pictures, for he could only

think of riding. He forgot that even the few pennies he made by selling his shell pictures helped to buy the things the family needed to live. Edgar forgot everything, except his love of the wonderful bike.

One evening Edgar walked up the road, tired from his day of riding. A small group was gathered in his front yard.

"They made it!" Thomas shouted.

"Boy! They made it for all of us," Martin shouted.

"Some show! Some show!" Mother was excited, too.

"Edgar, son, the Barbados bicycle team will be in the big European races. Just imagine that!"

"Even George St. Michael and his show-off self helped the team," Thomas added.

"Sure hope they find Cappie's practice wheel," Martin added. "Him being so superstitious and all, he is sure to go over there and blow it without that old bike."

Thumpity! Thumpity. Edgar's heart exploded in his chest.

"What bike?" Edgar asked.

"Cappie Whitehead's old practice thing. He does not like to ride a new racer, except for races. I guess that old wheel means plenty to him, having earned the money to buy the thing himself." Mrs. Bowen nodded her head knowingly.

"Where did he lose it?" Edgar asked softly, trying not to tremble.

"Never can tell," Thomas said. "Probably out good-timing and forgot all about his wheel. Hope he finds it. It's a good story for the paper."

"And something good to fall back on if he shouldn't show too well overseas." Mother was wise in such matters.

"Don't waste your talk on Edgar," Martin said. "He's too busy dreaming on his own bike to worry about Cappie's."

"Is the story in the paper?" Edgar asked.

"Dope! Dope! Of course it is in the paper. That's what mommy said." Thomas and Martin laughed.

Edgar disappeared into the house. He

GRE
YOUR

rushed through the story on the first page of the paper. He already knew it, but the words made it even more real for him. The bike he rode each day was Cappie's. He also knew he must return it.

So the next day, with slow and heavy steps, Edgar walked to Bridgetown, wheeling Cappie's bike. He no longer felt free to ride it. He hoped Cappie would not think he had taken the bike.

Edgar wheeled the bike through the repair section of Mr. Connell's shop. The store buzzed with excitement. Huge wooden crates took up the display space as workers moved everywhere, packing bikes for overseas shipping.

At first no one saw Edgar standing there. Finally a man, looking up, said, "Not today, son. We can't work on another bike today. These," he said pointing proudly, "belong to the boys of the Barbados team, and they must be crated to go by tomorrow. And that includes all repairs and spare parts."

"Hi, Edgar," said Mr. Connell as he came

into the work area. "And what brings you . . ." He could not finish the question. His eyes had caught sight of the bike. "That's Cappie's bike, boy child! Where did you find it?"

Edgar squeezed his eyes shut to hold back the tears and to try to frame the words to answer Mr. Connell's question in his mind. *There is no happiness*, he thought, *in being honest*.

Suddenly, there was a flash of memories, and Edgar couldn't answer. He stood, feeling the winds of Bathsheba whip against his legs and listened to the whispers of the leaves as they rustled in the night air in the cove. He remembered the big talk of the Americans at the airport as they flagged cabs to take them to their big hotels. He wanted to hold on to the memories, even though he could no longer hold on to the bike.

"Here they come!" The buzz ran from the front of the store to the back, from the salesroom to the repair shop and out to the garage. "It's the team!"

Edgar's heart began to pound. Sounds of laughter filled Edgar's ears. What could he say to Cappie? How could he explain how he, Edgar, had found the bike? Without a look over his shoulder, he could recognize the steady rhythm of Cappie's footsteps. *Pride*, he thought, *fills more pots on this island than food.*

Edgar forced his eyes to open, to look around at the workroom. The walls were lined with pegboard on which hooks had been fastened to hold bicycle parts of every possible description. And he saw the team. The whole team had stopped a few feet away from where he stood in the work area, their backs toward him.

But it was on Cappie Whitehead that Edgar's eyes locked. Cappie was a born leader, and now, standing so close to his hero, Edgar began to compare him with the heroes of his history books and of his story-

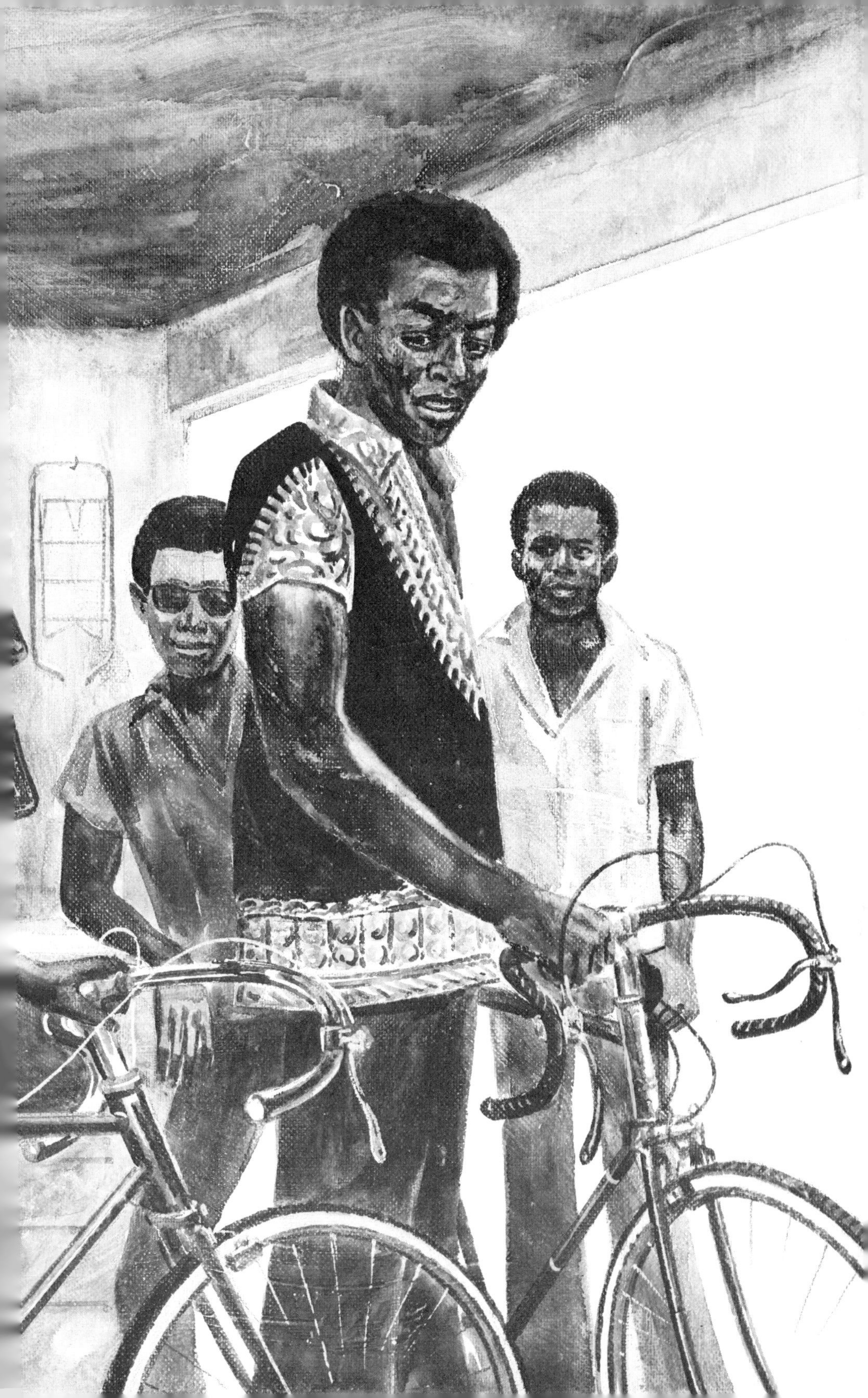

books. None were so great, so fine. For Cappie was dark in color, with fierce spires of wooly black hair framing his face, and he was of the salt and sand and earth of this small island, Barbados.

"Everything go, Connell?" Cappie Whitehead stopped strutting to ask while he continued to flex the muscles of his legs.

"Just about."

"Is my new bike all together for a test run?" Cappie asked, looking at the racks and racks of new bikes.

"Yes, it is, Cappie," said Mr. Connell. He wheeled the new racer out. The other men on the team crowded around, touching and patting it for luck.

"You've done your best, man. And I guess it will go," said Cappie. "But I know this new practice bike will not bring me the luck of Old Champ."

Edgar heard his words. He held his breath. The muscles of his chest felt like the steel bands of a crate being tightened by the strong grip of a mighty man.

"You mean," Mr. Connell asked, "if you

had Old Champ, you wouldn't want this?"

"Connell, man," said Cappie, "if I had Old Champ, you could throw this new thing away and I would still pay for it. Only Old Champ can show me the way on a new road. I know Old Champ, and Old Champ knows me!"

"Well," said Connell, "I guess you are a winner in many ways, Cappie." Connell pushed Edgar forward with the bike.

"Old Champ!" Cappie looked at Edgar, who could not let the bike go. "Did you find it?" he asked.

Edgar nodded his head, afraid the tears would spill out of his eyes. The days of freedom once again flashed in his mind, and he swallowed hard to keep down the lump in his throat.

Cappie Whitehead looked closely at Edgar. "I," he said softly "was once a boy with my own dreams. I see that look now in your eyes. When I was coming along, each mouth to feed was a burden. Those were lean, lean days for this island. Such things," gently he rubbed the chrome of the handlebars of Old

Champ, "were impossible, especially for a child."

"Hard times are plentiful still," Edgar said.

Cappie shouted. "Connell, give my new bike to this manchild. And ride it well, boy. For it is a wheel from Bridgetown, and they are the best!"

Dawn C. Thomas, author of *A Tree For Tompkins Park, Downtown Is*, and a half dozen other books, lives with her family at the Jersey shore. A mother, educator, and fighter for many causes, Dawn's stories reflect her varied childhood memories of Harlem, Brooklyn, and Barbados.

Don Miller was born in Jamaica and raised in Montclair, New Jersey. A graduate of Cooper Union, Mr. Miller has illustrated over thirty books as well as numerous magazine articles and several film strips. Currently, a selection of Don's paintings are on view, together with eight other artists, at The Museum of Natural History in *The Children of Africa* exhibit.